My Grandfather's House

by Bruce Coville · pictures by Henri Sorensen

BridgeWater Books

Text copyright © 1996 by Bruce Coville.
Illustrations copyright © 1996 by Henri Sorensen.

Published by BridgeWater Books, an imprint and trademark
of Troll Communications L.L.C.

Printed in the United States of America.

10   9   8   7   6   5   4   3   2   1

Library of Congress Cataloging-in-Publication Data

Coville, Bruce.
My grandfather's house / by Bruce Coville; illustrated by Henri Sorensen.
p.   cm.
Summary: When a child feels the cool, smooth fingers of his dead grandfather, he
finally understands that Grampa no longer lives in the house that was his body.
ISBN 0-8167-3804-1
[1. Grandfathers—Fiction.   2. Death—Fiction.]   I. Sorensen, Henri, ill.
II. Title.
PZ7.C8344My   1996   [E]—dc20   95-3630

For my four grandfathers, Fred, Luther, John, and Leonard—B.C.

To Erhard Jacobsen with thanks—H.S.

This used to be my grandfather's house.
But Grampa doesn't live here anymore.

I loved my grandfather.
He took me for long walks in the woods.

He knew how to make willow twigs into whistles.

He could even pull coins from behind my ear.

But he can't do those things anymore, because now he is gone.
When my parents told me Grampa was gone, I got mad. I wanted to
know where he went—and why he didn't take me with him.

"You don't understand," said my mother. "Your grandfather is dead. He died last night."

I started to cry.

Later, after I was done crying, I went to look for my mother. She was changing my sister's diaper.

"Where did Grampa go when he died?" I asked.

"I don't know," my mother answered. She looked like she was going to cry herself.

"Why don't you know?" I asked, feeling scared.

"Nobody knows for sure where you go when you die. But I can tell you what I think. I don't think Grampa has stopped being. I think he has gone to another place."

"What other place?"

She shook her head and said, "I don't know." Her voice sounded funny. She handed me the baby. "Watch Pook for a minute," she told me. Then she went into her bedroom.

I played with Pook. But all the time I was thinking of Grampa. I wanted to go find him. Only I didn't know if I wanted to go to that other place or not.

After supper I asked my father if he knew where Grampa had gone.

When he got a sad look on his face, I said, "Don't cry! Just tell me where he is."

My father closed his eyes. "Your grandfather went where we all go when we die," he said at last.

"But where is that?"

He shook his head. I could see that he didn't know.

I went next door to see my friend Mike. "Where do people go when they die?" I asked him.

"They go to the graveyard."

Now I was really confused. And scared, too. I had seen the graveyard. But I had never seen anybody there.

I wanted to go for a walk. Only I couldn't go into the woods without Grampa. So I climbed a tree instead. I sat in the branches and tried to think. Nothing made any sense.

Later I found a willow twig. I tried to make it into a whistle to call my grandfather home. But I didn't know how. Grampa hadn't taught me yet.

I went back inside and tried to pull a coin from behind Pook's ear. But I couldn't make the trick work. Grampa had never showed me the way to do it.

The next day my parents made me dress up. We took Pook to the baby-sitter. Then we drove to a big white house called a funeral home, to see Grampa one last time.

I was confused again. I couldn't understand how we could see him if he was gone.

"You'll have to be quiet in the funeral home," said my father.

He was right. Inside the home everyone walked softly and talked in whispers. It was so quiet it was frightening.

I didn't see any other children. I did see a lot of old people. Some of them were crying, which made me want to cry, too.

"Let's go see your grandfather," said my father.

He led me into a big room. At one end of the room was a long, shiny wooden box surrounded by a wall of flowers—more flowers than I had ever seen indoors. The sweet smell made my stomach twist a little.

My father said the box was called a coffin. He said my grandfather was inside it.

I felt funny.

My father took my hand. I held on tight. Together we walked to the coffin.

Dad was right. My grandfather was inside. He had on a suit and tie. His eyes were closed. His hands were folded across his chest.

But something was missing. This was not really my grandfather. The Grampa I knew was soft and wrinkly. This Grampa looked smooth and hard, and some of his wrinkles were gone.

My father took my hand in his. Then he put it on Grampa's hand. Grampa's fingers felt cool and smooth, not warm like they should have.

Finally I understood.

This used to be my grandfather's house.

But Grampa doesn't live here anymore.

Someday I will leave my house behind, just like my grandfather did. When that happens, I will go to look for him, because I love him very much.

I don't think it will happen for a long time.

And I don't worry about it now, because I know the house I live in isn't me.

I am not the house.

Someday I will know more.

But that's enough for now.

CORAZON AQUINO
President of the Philippines

by Emilie U. Lepthien

 CHILDRENS PRESS®

CHICAGO

Crowd cheers as military pilots and commanders
defect and join the Aquino supporters.

Library of Congress Cataloging-in-Publication Data
Lepthien, Emilie U. (Emilie Utteg)
   Corazon Aquino, president of the Philippines.
   (Picture-story biographies)
   Summary: A biography of the shy wife of a senator,
who after chaotic events in the Philippines, became
President of four million people on more than one
thousand islands.
      1. Aquino, Corazon Cojuangco—Juvenile literature.
2. Philippines—Presidents—Biography—Juvenile
literature.
[1. Aquino, Corazon Cojuangco. 2. Philippines—
Presidents]
I. Title. II. Series.
DS686.616.A65.L46 1987 959.9'047'0924 [B] [92]
87-14030   ISBN 0-516-04170-3

PHOTO CREDITS

AP/Wide World Photos, Inc.—4, 9 (2 photos),
   10 (left), 13, 15, 21 (2 photos), 22, 23 (left),
   24, 25 (2 photos), 27 (right), 28, 30
Courtesy Corazon Aquino—32
Picture Group:
   © Greg Smith—1, 3
   © Keystone, Paris—7, 14
Reuters/Bettmann Newsphotos—2, 10 (right), 11,
   16 (2 photos), 18, 19, 20, 23 (right), 26, 27
   (left), 29

Corazon Aquino greets eager supporters
along the campaign trail.

"Cory! Cory! Cory!" At every
rally people shouted her name. She
had become the leader many
Filipino people had been waiting
for. Finally, they had someone in
government they could trust.

When Corazon Aquino had
registered as a candidate for
president of the Philippines, she
listed her occupation as "housewife."

Mrs. Aquino shows election documents to reporters as she formally files her candidacy for president at the Commission on Elections, December 11, 1985.

Less than three months later, on February 25, 1986, the quiet, 53-year-old grandmother was sworn in as its seventh president.

Corazon Aquino was born on January 25, 1933, the sixth of eight children in the Cojuangco family. Cory grew up on the family's sugar plantation in Tarlac Province on Luzon, fifty miles north of Manila.

Like many Filipinos she is of Chinese, Malay, and Spanish descent.

The Cojuangco family was active in politics. Her father, Jose, and her brother served as congressmen. Her mother's family was involved in politics, too. Cory's maternal grandfather had been a vice-presidential candidate. Several uncles were senators and congressmen.

With her family background, it would not have been surprising if Cory had been interested in politics. But that was not the case, at least not until tragedy struck.

Cory attended a private Catholic school in Manila from 1938 to 1945. She enjoyed her studies and the religious atmosphere. Although she was shy, she was popular with her classmates. But her best friends were always her sisters: Josephine, Teresita, and Pacita.

In 1945 Cory enrolled in Assumption Convent High School. The following year she came to the United States and attended Ravenhill Academy in Philadelphia. She spent her junior and senior years at Notre Dame Convent School in New York.

After high school, Cory enrolled at Mount St. Vincent College in New York. She majored in French and mathematics. Already fluent in English and Tagalog, Cory also spoke some Spanish and Japanese.

Cory studied hard in college just as she had done in high school. At the end of each school year, she returned to the Philippines for vacation. One summer, following her junior year, she met a young journalist and law student from Tarlac Province. His name was

Benigno "Ninoy" Aquino.

During the summer Cory learned that she and Ninoy had many things in common.

In the fall, when Cory returned to college for her senior year, Ninoy began writing to her. After graduation from St. Vincent, Cory returned to Manila. She enrolled at Far Eastern University's Law School. But she completed only one semester. On October 11, 1959, she and Ninoy were married in Our

Lady of Sorrows Catholic Church in Pasay.

Before long, Ninoy became active in politics. He served as mayor and then as governor. In 1967 he became the only Liberal party candidate to be elected to the Senate. The Liberal party was trying to win more seats in the National Assembly so they could challenge the government of Ferdinand Marcos. Many people believed that the Marcos government was corrupt. It was destroying their freedom and making it impossible for democracy to exist in the Philippines. Ninoy and Cory believed this, too.

Throughout Ninoy's political career, Cory was at his side. She had become his strongest supporter. A friend once remarked that "Ninoy was the warrior. Cory polished his

Not long after Ferdinand Marcos (left) was sworn in as president of the Philippines in 1965, Ninoy and Cory (right) joined others in opposing his rule.

sword and took care of his horse." Although Cory seemed to remain in the background when Ninoy campaigned, she was a vital part of his career. He shared with Cory his concerns for the Philippines. He valued her opinion of right and wrong. Often he relied on her good judgment before making decisions.

Corazon Aquino poses with her children and grandchild (right) during
Christmas holidays in 1985. The picture of her husband Ninoy (left)
was taken in July 1983, a month before his death.

Over the years Cory and Ninoy
had five children—Maria Elena,
Aurora Corazon, Benigno III,
Victoria Elisa, and Kristian
Bernadette. The children kept Cory
very busy. Ninoy's political
activities kept her very involved.

In the 1971 elections, the Liberal
party won more seats in the
Assembly. Cory could see that her
husband was likely to become

president as soon as Marcos' final term ended in 1973. President Marcos also knew that Ninoy Aquino might be elected the next president. To prevent this threat to his government, Marcos imposed martial law (temporary rule by the military to control citizen unrest) in September 1972.

Many people who opposed the Marcos government were arrested. Ninoy was among the first to be jailed. For over seven and a half years he was kept in solitary

confinement. Faithfully, Cory
visited him several times a week.
She kept him in touch with the
Liberal party and carried messages
back and forth.

When President Marcos
permitted elections in 1978, Ninoy
ran as a candidate for the Assembly
from prison. Opposition candidates
running with him called their party
"Laban." It meant *Fight*. The
letters also stood for Tagalog words
meaning *People Force*.

Although Cory had no experience
in public speaking, she began
making political speeches for her
husband. Maria Elena, seven-year-
old Kristian, and young Benigno,
also spoke at rallies. President
Marcos did not like the Aquino
children campaigning for their
father. He said that a good mother
would not allow her children to

campaign. Cory replied, "The children will stop campaigning when Ninoy is released from prison." But Ninoy was not released.

Only after he suffered a heart attack was Ninoy allowed to fly to the United States for triple-bypass surgery. On May 8, 1980, the Aquino family left Manila for Texas.

Following Ninoy's successful surgery, they moved into a

Cory and Ninoy with three of their daughters.

comfortable home in Boston, Massachussetts. Cory spent three of the happiest years of her life there. While her husband lectured at several universities and planned for the overthrow of Marcos, she resumed her role as wife and mother.

In 1983, however, life changed. Ninoy decided to return to the Philippines to challenge Ferdinand Marcos. Cory knew that Ninoy would probably be arrested again, but she believed the country needed her husband. Cory agreed that she and the children would join Ninoy two weeks after he arrived in Manila.

But a terrible tragedy changed their plans. The moment Ninoy stepped off the plane in Manila, August 21, 1983, he was shot and killed. When Cory heard the heartbreaking news, she and the

Airport security men lift the lifeless body of Benigno Aquino into a security van. Aquino's assassin lies dead near the van.

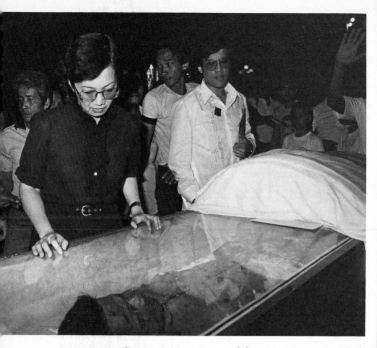

Corazon Aquino and her son Benigno (left)
stand beside the body of Ninoy. Two days
later, the funeral procession moved through
the streets of Manila (right) while
millions watched.

children sought comfort in church.
Prayer had always brought Cory
strength before. Now she would
have to rely on her faith to bring
her through this grief.

Several days later Cory and the
children flew to Manila for Ninoy's
funeral. Two million people
marched in the funeral procession.
Months later most of these

supporters looked to Cory for leadership. Several close friends and influential people convinced Cory to continue her husband's fight to return freedom and democracy to the Philippines.

In May 1984, parliamentary elections were scheduled. Many people knew that votes would not be counted properly. Those opposing Marcos suggested boycotting the elections. But Cory urged everyone to vote. As a result, opposition candidates won a third of the Assembly seats.

Although the constitution did not call for a presidential election at this time, Marcos called for a "snap" election to take place on February 7, 1986. Since several candidates would be running against him, he thought he would win. But the opposition outsmarted him. They narrowed the number of candidates to one.

Corazon Aquino received a million petitions promising support if she would run against Marcos. After several days of prayer, Cory accepted the will of God voiced by her people. She decided to run.

Immediately, Cory convinced Salvador Laurel, who was planning his own campaign against Marcos, to run as vice-president with her.

Corazon Aquino shows the Laban (Fight) sign as she leads her followers in "Bayan Ko," the theme song of the opposition.

Filipinos wave yellow flags and ribbons to welcome
Corazon Aquino and Salvador Laurel in the city of Cebu.

With only six weeks left to
campaign, and limited funds, the
two began an almost impossible
task. Often they worked 16-hour
days flying from island to island.
Hundreds of volunteers began
distributing Cory banners, bumper
stickers, buttons, and yellow T-shirts.

Whenever Cory was in public she
dressed in yellow. She wanted to
remind voters of her husband's

19

Aquino campaigning in Baguio City, January 1985.

imprisonment and death. People
sang, "Tie A Yellow Ribbon" in his
memory. They raised their hands to
form an L for "Laban."

To make sure the election would
be honest, Cory's supporters
organized NAMFREL, National
Movement for Free Elections.
Thousands of volunteers served as
poll watchers. The United States
sent observers to help insure an
honest election.

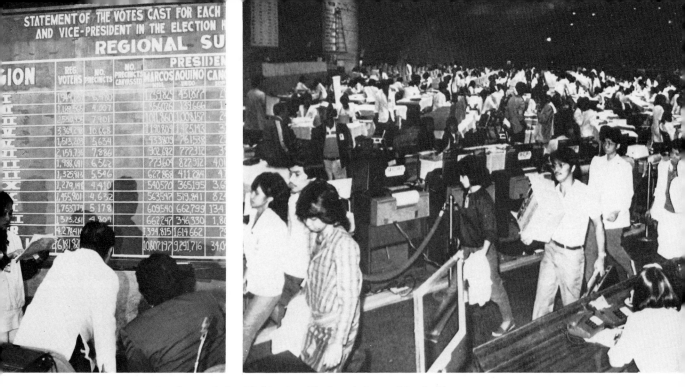

Members of the Philippine National Assembly (left)
examine the final election results. At the
Commission on Elections' national tabulation center
(right), workers walk out to protest vote fraud.

But President Marcos still
controlled the National Assembly.
On election day, when the
Assembly announced the results, he
was declared the winner. Some
Assembly members walked out,
claiming vote fraud.

In NAMFREL's count, Corazon
Aquino had received a plurality of
almost 800,000 votes. Ignoring the

widespread cheating by Marcos supporters, Cory declared herself the winner. Quickly she made her position known. "This is my message to Mr. Marcos and his puppets. Do not threaten Cory Aquino, because I am not alone."

On February 16, Cory and Laurel held a "Triumph of the People" rally in Manila. Between one-and-a-half-and two-million people attended. Cory asked the people to join in nonviolent

Those opposed to Marcos demonstrate near the presidential palace.

The Aquino administration got underway in a spirit of peace and harmony. Corazon with Jaime Cardinal Sin (left). Juan Ponce Enrile and General Fidel Ramos (right)

protests and boycotts. Once again the people responded.

Cory and Laurel flew to Cebu City for another rally. On February 22, they received word of a military revolt against Marcos. Leading the rebellion were Defense Minister Juan Ponce Enrile and Lieutenant General Fidel V. Ramos.

On the radio Jaime Cardinal Sin, head of the Roman Catholic Church in the Philippines, called on

23

Army tanks stopped by a wall of people.

the people to support the soldiers opposing Marcos. Hundreds of thousands responded. They filled the streets near the army camps.

General Ver, a Marcos supporter, ordered tanks to attack the rebel soldiers in the camps. People knelt down in the streets and prayed as the tanks approached. The soldiers in the tanks did not want to fire on their own countrymen and women. Instead the tanks turned around.

Marcos campaigning with his vice-presidential running mate,
Arturo Tolentino (left), and speaking from the palace balcony
after his self-proclaimed victory (right).

Meanwhile in Cebu City, Cory
appealed to President Marcos to
step down. Ronald Reagan, the
president of the United States, also
asked him to resign. But Marcos
refused.

On February 25, 1986, two
presidential inaugurations took
place. At 10:45 A.M. at Club Filipino,

Dona Aurora Aquino, Cory's
mother-in-law, held the bible as
Cory took the oath of office as the
seventh president of the Republic of
the Philippines.

Cory's inaugural address was
brief. Then she asked everyone to
join in singing the Lord's Prayer.
When they sang "My Native Land"
they raised their hands to form the
familiar L for "Laban."

At noon Ferdinand Marcos was
also inaugurated. But by 9:30 that

Two days after Marcos appeared on television (left) to assure Filipinos that his presidency was secure, he and his family were flown to Hawaii (right), where they remain in exile.

evening Marcos, his family, and friends (including General Ver) left Malacanang Palace for Clark Air Force Base. Under pressure from the United States, Marcos and his supporters went into exile in Hawaii.

Getting Ferdinand Marcos to step down as president solved only one problem. More difficult ones followed. Corazon faced tremendous problems as the new president. The nation was deeply in debt. Unemployment was high and seventy percent of the people lived in poverty. The Communist New People's Army and the Muslims in Mindanao threatened the peace.

President Aquino knew major reforms were necessary. But how were they to be accomplished? Land needed to be distributed more equally among all the people. Millions, perhaps even billions, of dollars that Marcos and his friends

President Aquino presiding over her first Cabinet meeting

Members of Aquino's cabinet pose on the steps of the Malacanang Palace.

had taken from the country while they were in power had to be returned. Only then could needed programs be financed to improve conditions. Finally, all the opposition groups in the Philippines had to be united.

One of the first things Corazon Aquino did as president was to call for a new constitution. "It is for our children," she said, "so that they can live in freedom, so that we shall never have another dictator."

On February 2, 1987, the new
constitution was approved. It
assured that Mrs. Aquino would
remain in office until 1992. Civil
rights were guaranteed also. Then
on May 11, elections were held for
the Senate, the House of
Representatives, and for local
officials. With few exceptions
Aquino-endorsed candidates won
the elections.

Since her election, Corazon
Aquino has refused to live in
Malacanang Palace. She does not

want to repeat the excesses of the former president. Instead, she wants all citizens to share in the wealth of the country. She wants the government to provide an opportunity for every citizen to have a job and a decent way of life.

If President Aquino can restore stability in the Philippines, provide jobs for people, and reform land distribution, she will have fulfilled her husband's dream. Only the future can tell us if she will do these things.

Corazon Aquino has already made her mark on history. Not only will she be remembered as the quiet woman who "polished Ninoy's sword and took care of his horse." A greater tribute follows. She has bravely taken up the sword of the fallen warrior. Now she rides his horse in battle.

CORAZON COJUANGCO AQUINO

TIME LINE

1933	January 25 born in Tarlac Province, Philippines
1938-45	Attends elementary school at St. Scholastica's College
1945	Freshman at Assumption Convent High School
1946-47	Leaves with family for United States; attends Ravenhill Academy
1947-49	Junior and senior years at Notre Dame Convent School
1949-53	Earns Bachelor of Arts degree at Mount St. Vincent College
1954	October 11, 1954 marries Benigno Aquino
1954-72	Housewife and mother of five children
1972	September, begins thrice weekly visits to Benigno in prison
1978	Campaigns for her jailed husband
1980	May 8, Benigno is released from prison; family flies to U.S.
1980-83	Housewife again in Newton, Massachusetts, suburb of Boston, while Benigno lectures at Harvard University and Massachusetts Institute of Technology
1983	August 21, Benigno assassinated at Manila Airport
1984	Receives honorary doctorate degree from Mount St. Vincent College; receives other honorary distinctions from other schools, religious and professional associations
1984	May, urges citizens to vote in parliamentary election
1985	October, asked to run for presidency
1985	December 3, files her candidacy for presidency
1985	December 16, begins nationwide campaign
1986	February 7, Election Day
1986	February 25, takes oath of office as seventh president of the Republic of the Philippines
1987	February 2, voters approve new constitution; August, the government puts down revolt by pro-Marcos military troops, the fifth revolt since Corazon Aquino took office.

To Emilie Lepthien,
With my good wishes!
Cory Aquino
Nov. 17, 1986

President Aquino sent this autographed picture to the author, Emilie Lepthien.

ABOUT THE AUTHOR

EMILIE UTTEG LEPTHIEN earned a BS and MA degree and a certificate in school administration from Northwestern University. She has worked as an upper grade science and social studies teacher supervisor and a principal of an elementary and upper grade center for twenty years. Ms. Lepthien also has written and narrated science and social studies scripts for the Radio Council of the Chicago Board of Education.

Ms. Lepthien was awarded the American Educator's Medal by Freedoms Foundation. She is a member of the Delta Kappa Gamma Society International, Chicago Principals Association, and life member of the NEA. She has been a co-author of primary social studies texts for Rand, McNally and Co. and an educational consultant for Encyclopaedia Britannica Films. Ms. Lepthien has written Enchantment of the World books on Australia, Ecuador, Iceland, and the Philippines.